MR. DAYDREAM
and the big splash

Original concept
by Roger Hargreaves

Illustrated and written by
Adam Hargreaves

KU-327-178

Mr Happy was not feeling his usual happy self.

He had been waiting at the bus stop for half an hour. And it was raining.

Suddenly someone tapped him on the arm. He turned round to find a small blue figure standing beside him.

"Hello, I'm Mr Daydream."

"Hello," said Mr Happy. "I'm Mr Happy."

"I know," said Mr Daydream. "It's not much fun here, shall we go somewhere else?"

"That would be nice," said Mr Happy.

Mr Daydream whistled.

As if by magic, which it may or may not have been, a red bus appeared at the bus stop.

There were other people on the bus. Mr Grumpy, Mr Sneeze, Mr Bump, and Mr Tickle were all there.

"Where shall we go?" asked Mr Daydream.

"Somewhere where it doesn't rain," cried Mr Grumpy.

Mr Daydream started the engine and drove along the road. To Mr Happy's astonishment, the bus began to rise into the air.

They were flying!

They landed with a bump.

"Ow!" cried Mr Bump, falling off his seat.

They all trouped off the bus to find they were on a sand dune surrounded, as far as they could see, by more sand dunes.

"This is too dry!" moaned Mr Grumpy.

There was no pleasing Mr Grumpy.

They all boarded the bus again.

"Where to next?" asked Mr Daydream.

"Somewhere soft," said Mr Bump, rubbing his head which he had bumped climbing back onto the bus.

They flew to the North Pole where the snow was so deep that as much as he fell over, Mr Bump could not hurt himself.

Not surprisingly, Mr Grumpy thought it was too cold and he was not the only one.

"**ATISHOO!**" sneezed Mr Sneeze.

"Can we go somewhere **ATISHOO!** hot?" asked Mr Sneeze.

They flew to the South American Jungle.

Mr Sneeze loved it.

He no longer had a cold.

There was also something else he no longer had. Can you see what had changed about him?

"This is too hot," moaned Mr Grumpy – some things never change.

"I'd like to go somewhere ticklish," said Mr Tickle.

Mr Daydream had to think hard about this one, but eventually they landed on a great plain where the grass grew tall enough to tickle your nose.

"Ha, ha . . . I, he he . . . hate, ha, ha, ha . . . this," laughed Mr Grumpy.

"Now, where would you like to go, Mr Happy?" asked Mr Daydream.

"Somewhere where we would all be happy. I know, a tropical island resort," said Mr Happy.

In no time at all, Mr Happy was lying on a lilo in a pool beneath a palm tree, bathed in sunlight.

He sighed happily.

And so did Mr Tickle and Mr Sneeze and Mr Daydream.

Everyone was happy. Even Mr Grumpy!

Well, almost.

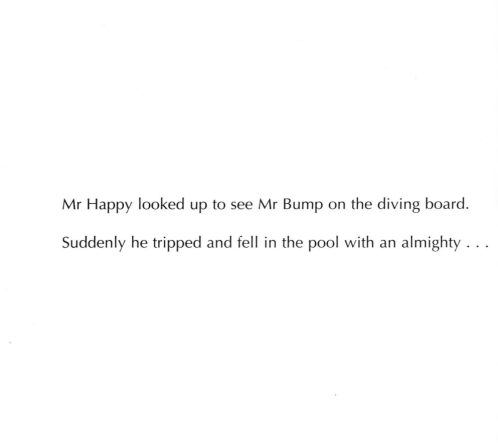

Mr Happy looked up to see Mr Bump on the diving board.

Suddenly he tripped and fell in the pool with an almighty . . .

. . . **SPLASH!**

Mr Happy opened his eyes.

The number 10 bus had splashed a puddle all over him.

He was back at the bus stop!

No more pool.

No more palm trees.

No more sunshine.

It had all been a daydream!

"Hurry up," said someone behind him.

"This is too wet!"

Now, I wonder who that could be?